TOMES OF ZINKA

Angel Kings Trinity
Volume I: Bloodline
Volume II: Ancient
Volume III: Angel Wars

Savage Sector Trinity
Volume IV: Caecorum Rex
Volume V: Last Valander
Volume VI: Triage

Origins Trinity
Volume X: Welvox
Volume XI: Swords of Power
Volume XII: Killer Company

Gloom Kings Trinity
Volume XIII: Niefax
Volume XIV: Star Eater
Volume XV: Genesis

D1525252

Fantasy by Alexandra Edgeworth

GRAPHIC TOMES
Bloodline GT1
Bloodline GT2

COLLECTIONS
Wings of the Yaverse
Voices of Two Worlds: A Collection of Poetry from
Earth and Zinka
Yaverse Studio

NOVELS
Vast of Wolves
Shadow Empire
DarkTime Complex: Zenith Origins
Possessor
Darksiders
Swirl
Saberog
Toxic Vein
Fire Psychic
Cyrenthia
Red Jester
Bastille
Attack the Sun
Map Drop
Psycho Star

ALEXANDRA EDGEWORTH

MATER VES

YAVERSE

Mater Ves
A Yaverse Book
First Edition, 2022

Yaverse and Yaverse Books are property of Yaverse Books.
www.yaverse.com

When the unclean spirit is gone out of a man, he walketh through dry places, seeking rest, and findeth none. Then he saith, I will return into my house from whence I came out; and when he is come, he findeth it empty, swept, and garnished. Then goeth he, and taketh with himself seven other spirits more wicked than himself, and they enter in and dwell there; and the last state of that man is worse than the first. Even so shall it be also unto this wicked generation.

—**Matthew 12:43-45,** *KJV*

Outpost Mission 882
Entry 3: Debriefing Summary

Yellow boots covered in caution tape scuff marks walk through a crowded building. The gait is steady, strong, and unflinching, which sends red pointy heels and black dress shoes running. The clatter of fancy shoes halts, the echoes of superiority cease, and even the wolf pack clamor snuffs out like a parlor trick candle. Glinting, worn spurs and steel toe bracers catch the eye better than a sparkling time device that swallowed an entire shift's pay. Only the ring of sawblade spurs fills the now silent lobby as the man attached to them finally pauses at the lobby desk.

The man behind the desk panics as he sorts through papers and electronic reporting files, but the yellow-booted fiend appears as stone. No one can see him breathe behind his iridescent blue flak jacket. No one sees him reaching for the combat knife with the neon green handle strapped to his upper left leg. No one sees his face behind one of the most sophisticated pieces of Outpost technology since Zenith invasion.

Rising like fox ears, the helmet has two sound detection antennae with reinforced metallic panels to prevent external force damage. Eyes work unseen behind a neon purple visor that changes colors based on indoor or outdoor environment lighting. The snout of the helmet looks more like a medieval helm with a blackout grid mouthpiece to intimidate the enemy.

It's working.

A woman opens a side door to the lobby and stares out at the other guests who now huddle behind fake plants or under upholstered couches. She drags her finger in the air at the scary man and says, "He will see you now, sir."

The spurs ring as the man in yellow boots strides to the open door, the woman carefully moves aside, and she quietly shuts the door behind him. After locking the door, the woman doubles her pace to catch up to the man.

"Sir," she says and lifts her right sleeve. On her forearm is an electronic band with computational abilities. She appears to use it for setting meetings and reviewing notes. She taps through a few files and says, "Sir, you're report on Mission 882 requires further explanation in two paragraphs."

The man continues to walk without a sound.

"Um, I have here," she says, "that you located the survey team and, I quote, 'dealt with the surveyor who stole the native's possessions.' Can you elaborate on *dealt with*?"

The man exhales through his helmet, which sounds like a diesel truck, and says, "Thou shalt not steal."

The woman turns a few shades paler. "Very well. Uh, I also have here in the report that you say, 'Dr. Oduk was found guilty of idolatry when he succumbed to the native's desire for someone on the team to pay respects to their rock.' Can you elaborate…on *found guilty*?"

"Thou shalt have no other gods before me."

They reach another closed door guarded by two men in simple armor, but they quickly remove themselves from the shadow of this approaching mercenary. The doors open, the woman leaves, and the man in yellow boots walks inside and stands still until the doors shut behind him.

At the other end of the long, bleak room with only four windows along one wall is a small desk where a busy man hunkers into his seat as he works on seven touchscreen monitors. Occasionally, he will write something down on a piece of scratch paper from a pile of scavenged paper he has found from around the city.

Outside the nearest window is a megacity, at least ten stories high, and the sun blinks through the heavy clouds to reveal the worn sky road traffic lights that barely have enough solar power to keep hovering in place.

The man behind the desk sighs, folds two of his screens shut, and looks up at the mercenary. He quickly grabs his forest green hat, shoves it over his messy hair, and stands. Walking over to the other man, he holds out his hand and says, "Welcome back from that mud hole, Rosek."

Rosek stares at the man. "Wendin."

Wendin smirks, lowers his hand, and shoves his hands in his pockets as he walks over to the nearest window. "I'm closing the file on Mission 882. Those people couldn't help the Outpost better than a can of worms. They almost sacrificed one of our surveyors to a cluster of rocks."

Rosek is silent.

"I fear the Outpost is losing its original purpose," Wendin says and stares down at the traffic. "We're looking for things to help our coalition of planets to fight against the Zeniths, not take on more people who the Zeniths won't even bother to invade. The Zeniths want developed planets with advanced weapons and knowledge. They like to play with their food before they eat it, but I'm not telling you something you don't already know."

Rosek only turns his head to Wendin.

"I have a serious issue developing in the farthest sector of Outpost territory space," Wendin says and sighs. "You're the only man I know that can finally put it to rest."

Rosek remains silent.

Wendin turns around and says, "There's a planet with high levels of Grakinium where we sent pioneers to initially study the best place for mining, but they did not report back. We then sent a survey team to locate and complete the task, but they only reported once before never reporting again. I need you to safeguard my new survey team and bring them home when the job is done."

Rosek flexes and says, "How many?"

"It's the usual five-person survey team," Wendin says. "One man on the team is the last Hynibrian and an indispensable asset to the Outpost. I had the honor of meeting him before his planet was destroyed by Zeniths. I need you to take priority in his protection. The others are valuable and, quite honestly, the best ones we have left."

"Planetary information?"

"Not much," Wendin says and walks over to his desk. He grabs a few pieces of paper and says, "From what little reporting I received from the previous teams, I can only say there is breathable air, to an extent, and no signs of life. I'm hoping this is merely a radiation issue from the Grakinium, which is why we will be supplying you and your team the proper attire to combat radiation poisoning."

"Risk level?"

"Low, I think," Wendin says. "There will be a forensic pathologist on the team this time to confirm radiation as the cause, but I want you to exercise extreme caution if that's ruled out. There may be a biological pathogen, and, if that's the case, the team medic should be able to confirm. You will also have a mechanic, a cartographer, and an archaeologist."

Rosek shakes his head.

"This archaeologist won't upset you," Wendin says. "He's a good man and a former Zenith survivor, like yourself. Though I will say…that is where your commonalities end. He's a Wild Rote from the extinct Planet Dulkor."

Rosek sighs through his helmet. "Enough said."

"Very well," Wendin says and walks up to Rosek with a packet of metal cards. "Here are their background files. The Cold Rib file was not easy to procure, but I know you have your requirements before accepting a job. I also have your weapon supplies and ship docking card in there. Your team will meet you at the docking station. Something tells me they'll know you when they…see you."

Rosek takes the packet and starts reading the files.

"You know," Wendin says, "you and I are the only men I know still interested in paper trails."

Rosek looks up from the files. "Paper is civilized."

Outpost Mission 883
Entry 12: Team Mission Briefing

Giant machines fill the long docking bay as hundreds of ships, small and colossal, lock into the ports or clank against the magnetic hull clamps. The walkway is narrow, only enough room for eight bodies across, and the upper levels are dedicated solely to shipping crates and goods. A thin, black rail guards all departing and arriving people from falling down eighteen stories into the lower city levels, but a small sign hangs from a dingy rope that reads *Fall at Your Own Risk.*

Near one of the support columns, halfway down the docking hall, is a young man in an orange, plastic coat that goes all the way down to his knees. The rest of his attire is black, as is his hair, and he carries a bundle of sealed, waterproof pipes in a bag on his back. In his lap is his small satchel that carries a unique set of pens and pencils, compasses and grid makers, protractors and oddities that provide him a decent living. In his callus-infested right hand is a small pencil, shaven down to nearly the eraser, and he sketches the docking bay with almost lifelike qualities.

He hears a bang from one of the ships, pauses in his sketch, and straightens. His eyes are thin, but they glow with a goldfish glean, and his cheeks protrude to the point that they exit the skin with a tangerine sheen to mark his maturity for his species. He spies a woman in grey walking down the docks.

She wears layers of tight grey and blue as her blond hair slides over her left shoulder in a thick, tight braid. She brings only one bag, a dark and ominous bag with a lock, and on her hip is the standard sidearm of most Outpost contractors. As she walks closer, the orange-boned man realizes that she's not wearing grey…she *is* grey. Her attire is cerulean, but her skin puts off the appearance of someone who died weeks ago. Her most striking features are her bright, red lips and hazel eyes. If she were to close her eyes and suck in her lips, she might as well be dead.

The woman halts and stares at the man. "Are you…with the Outpost?"

"Yes, uh, yes," the man says and stashes away his drawings in a folder. He tucks the folder under his arm as he stands and holds out his hand. "I'm Xool, the Cartographer."

"Yalena," she says and refuses to shake his hand. "Forensics."

"Oh," Xool says and awkwardly sits back down. "That makes sense."

Yalena raises a black eyebrow. "Why?"

Xool clears his throat. "No reason, I guess. Ahem! Well, have you uh, met the rest of the team?"

"No. You're the first impression."

Xool makes a nervous laugh as a magnifying glass falls out of his pocket. He scrambles to pick it up and almost falls over from his seated position. He quickly straightens and says, "Yikes then, right? I'm not good with people."

"I only work with dead ones."

Xool presses his lips thin. "Looks like you beat me."

Yalena frowns.

Suddenly, a muscular man in an armored bodysuit walks up to them. He slings a giant work bag over his shoulder as a long, thin stick hangs from his mouth. The reinforced metal plates over his muscles add to his robotic demeanor, but his rugged face covered in random scorch scars clearly suggests his occupation. His hair sticks straight up, his long ears do the same, and his black eyes seem to grin with his sharp teeth. He glances to Xool and Yalena before removing the stick from between two fangs.

"You smell like death, woman," the man says. "You must be the cadaver girl."

Yalena glares at him. "And you the Mech."

"Yeap," he says and nods to them. "Mech Master Ptol at your service. If it's broke…that's because I hadn't touched it yet."

Xool swallows hard and says, "G-good one."

Ptol studies Xool. "What's wrong with your face?

"Oh," Xool says and offers a nervous laugh. "No worries. I'm not offended, but—"

"Don't care."

"Right," Xool says. "There's actually nothing, uh, technically wrong with my visage. I'm a Xo'wak. We all look like this."

"What? Like you've been punched by a fruit?"

Yalena sighs and puts her bag down by her feet.

Xool shrugs and makes a silly smile. "I guess so!"

Ptol cracks a laugh, slaps Xool on the shoulder, and says, "I'm just messing with you! Whoa, you're all bony under there. Won't catch a lady that way, unless your dead, and then she'll take care of you."

"No," Yalena says and sighs. "Different department."

Xool makes a forced grin. "I uh, don't make enough to get meat credits. It's a substance I've learned to go without."

"Shame," Ptol says and turns his head. "Oh great. Here comes a creep."

Walking down the docking hall is a man in a red bodysuit built lean and nimble. His white hair sits high and tight along his head as red ears curl out with two points. His eyes are also red and the tips of his fingers look like he picked an entire cherry tree before he arrived. Carrying no pack or luggage, he carries only the necessities in several pouches along his black belt.

"Midday to you all," he says. "A gathering of this rarity must only be an Outpost team. Allow me to introduce myself. I am Arch Legathes and I will be serving as your medical attendant during this mission."

Ptol glares at him and says, "Arch?"

"Yes," Legathes says. "It is my title and rank among my people. It means I am clean in my spirit and am able to heal others without using resources that may take away from the needs of others."

Ptol shudders like someone crawled up into his spine.

Xool holds out his inky hand and says, "Nice to meet you, Legathes!"

Legathes smiles and shakes his hand.

Someone coughs and shoves by Xool, which sends him back into his seat, and he vehemently shakes Legathes' hand with a leather glove as his aviator goggles hug the top half of his face. He wears an old tunic with buttons up the center and he sports a pair of jeans. Yalena finally shows signs of life as she studies the man's rare pants.

"Excellent," the man says and looks over Legathes. "I thought the Zeniths snatched all of you. This is such a treat. I couldn't help but overhear…are you really an Arch?"

Legathes nods.

"Amazing," the man says and removes his goggles. Both Xool and Ptol jerk at the sight. The man's eyes are bright violet and his grin is pearly white. He laughs and says, "I'm Dr. Nekang. I too am a rare species these days, but I think people might be happy about that."

Legathes lowers his hand and says, "I'm sorry, I do believe I have heard your name before."

"Nah," Nekang says. "I did publish some papers on multiple identity disorders in post-Zenith populations a long time ago. Since then, my work mainly involves pre-Zenith cultural retro-studies to find possible Zenith triggers for arrival."

Ptol raises an eyebrow. "So, you study cultures to see why Zeniths attacked them?"

"You must be the Mech Master," Nekang says. "I'll be seeing you if any of my archaeological equipment malfunctions!"

Yalena's jaded expression finally softens as she senses the presence of another person nearby. She swiftly turns her head, which prompts the others in the group to do so, and that's when everyone sees Commander Rosek standing all the way at the other end of the docking hallway talking to the Dock Master. He still wears his helmet and all of his gear.

"Ah," Legathes says and smiles. "That would be Rosek. I was wondering if I would ever get the honor to work with him."

"Honor? Are you insane," Ptol says. "He's a killer. He'll snap you in half if you do the wrong thing on a mission. If the Outpost hired him, then this job has serious issues."

"Rosek," Xool says. "Not *Commander* Rosek? The last Tide Man?"

"The same," Dr. Nekang says. "I heard he escaped Zenith capture…still in one piece."

"Yeah," Xool says and swirls a pen in the air. "I remember! It was all over the frequencies. He was found by Outpost mercenaries in an ejection pod. They're still trying to figure out the technology, but Rosek gave the Outpost so much information that the coalition was even able to exist in the first place."

Ptol presses his lips thin. "Rosek? *Made* the Outpost? Come on, kid."

"I have heard similar tales," Legathes says. "Rosek may not look it, but he is as old as the movement."

"A Tide Man," Ptol says and shrugs. "Looks like the Zeniths were after their longevity."

"Perhaps," Dr. Nekang says, "but it more likely has something to do with the rare abilities of Tide Folk. They were the best shipbuilders and swimmers, said to be able to hold their breath for one hour, and their ability to withstand large amounts of pressure made them perfect test subjects for deep space travel and stasis."

Yalena turns her attention to Dr. Nekang. "And you, Dr. Nekang?"

"Me? I'm merely a Wild Rote. As long as I keep my gloves on, no one gets hurt."

Yalena squints her eyes. "Isn't it *any* skin contact?"

Xool and Ptol take a step back.

Nekang shrugs and says, "I keep to myself. In case there is an incident, I brought plenty of antidote in my luggage."

Rosek is suddenly behind the group.

Yalena merely turns her head, picks up her bag, and says, "Commander Rosek. Please direct me to our ship. I am ready to go."

Rosek merely nods once and walks past the group. Yalena silently follows him, Dr. Nekang follows as he adjusts his gloves, and Ptol pats Xool on the shoulder.

"Between the two of us," Ptol says, "we're the most normal, Xool."

Xool blinks and looks up at Ptol. "Me? Normal?"

Ptol squints one side of his face for a second, which reveals his sharp teeth. "Eh, I mean…the most normal."

"Yeah," Xool says and smiles. "Normal."

Arch Legathes watches Ptol practically drag Xool along, like a little brother, and he studies how the group walks in line behind Rosek to a medium-sized warship in the back of the docking bay. Legathes slowly walks, strolls around families boarding the civilian vessels, waves to a bright-eyed child, and then he stops at the base of the ship ramp. Legathes reads the name, *Manifest*, and sighs.

Rosek steps out of the ship's shadows, walks down the ramp, and stands in front of Legathes. He breathes through his helmet and says, "Is there a problem?"

"I am a man of few complaints," Legathes says, "but I do have issue with this ship."

"Explain."

"The name bothers me."

"Agreed," Rosek says and turns around. "Board."

Legathes nods and follows Rosek onto the ship as the ramp slides back into the hull. The side door closes, Legathes enters the navigation room, and he sits in the back in the only empty seat.

Rosek enters the driver's seat as Ptol takes co-pilot while he runs a few ship diagnostics. Xool quickly straps in and starts checking the mission route map. Dr. Nekang sits apart from the team, by the hallway leading into the ship quarters, and he calmly pries open an old book to read. Yalena neatly sits beside Xool, her bag tucked under her seat, and she rests her hands in her lap as she stares off into oblivion. Legathes is the only one observing everyone and he cranes his neck to see Xool making adjustments to the route in a way that shortens the trip by days at a time.

The ship's engines activate, the docking bay disappears, and Rosek zooms out of the atmosphere before there is an opportunity to blink. After looking over Xool's corrections, Rosek signals everyone to rise and join him in the center of the room where a small obelisk waits. Once they all walk over, Rosek places his palm on the Outpost obelisk, it accepts his handprint, and a giant planet image appears.

"This is Mater Ves," Rosek says. He points to a dark splotch on the planet and the planet stops rotating. "This is where we received only one communication from the second survey team before total blackout. Our mission is to locate any bodies, logs, files, and usable equipment to finish the initial investigation of Mater Ves and provide cause of death for missing persons."

Yalena slowly turns her head to Rosek. "What if there are any surveyors still alive?"

"Unlikely," Rosek says. "Outpost Intelligence suggests radiation poisoning from high Grakinium deposits. The entire surface of the planet is made of the element."

Dr. Nekang raises his hand. "This is merely speculation, I presume? Grakinium was only recently discovered to have properties desirable in the latest computational devices."

"Grakinium, huh," Ptol says and folds his arms. "Even planets *not* part of the Outpost would be interested."

"Yeah," Xool says. "One chip can power an entire cargo vessel. If we found a planet made entirely of Grakinium, we'd be set against the Zeniths for sure!"

"Point being," Dr. Nekang says to Xool. "We are not sure if large amounts of Grakinium are radioactive because we have only tested on the available, small amounts."

"As a precaution," Rosek says. "We have suits. There is also speculation the air might be contaminated, an airborne pathogen, or an unknown animal lifeform may be responsible for the missing teams. Keep all of this in mind during your investigation."

Yalena folds her hands and says, "Rad suits are classified as sealed, so they can guard against air pollution and airborne pathogens if we use the recommended air cartridges."

Rosek nods and says, "If it's an animal, I will know. Any questions?"

Xool raises his hand. "You said there was only one communication, right? Do you have the log?"

Rosek nods and enters a few commands into the obelisk. The planet disappears and a square screen pops up with a woman's face. Her eyes are glittery green and her dark brown hair blows in a soft breeze. In her surveyor vest pocket is a small, metal-bound book with a heart pressed into the front. She starts to move around, as if she does not know she is recording herself, and two team members walk behind her with equipment bags.

"Kuressa," a team member says. "You're log is on."

"Oh! Oops," Kuressa says and stares at her screen. "Sorry, I'll—"

The log ends.

Ptol clears his throat and swallows. "That's grim."

"The air looks agreeable," Dr. Nekang says. "They show no symptoms of air or radiation poisoning."

"On the contrary, doctor," Yalena says. "There are latent symptoms for some pathogens, even some air toxins, but I will inspect the bodies, if there are any to be found. Remember, doctor, that I study the recently deceased, not you."

Dr. Nekang clears his throat. "Fair enough."

Yalena turns to Rosek. "May I be excused?"

Rosek nods. Yalena walks over to her seat, grabs her bag, and leaves the navigation room towards the sleeping quarters. Once she is out of sight, they all still hear her stomping to a door, and then they hear her slam the door shut.

Rosek turns to the rest of the group. "Any questions?"

Legathes offers a slow nod and says, "If we find survivors, Commander Rosek, I request full authority over their wellness and recovery."

Rosek nods. "Granted."

Legathes puts a calm hand over his chest, offers a slight bow, and dismisses himself. Dr. Nekang briskly leaves as Ptol turns to Rosek.

"So," Ptol says. "I found a few chinks in the armor. This ship has ventilation errors and engine bubbles."

Rosek turns his helmet to Ptol. "Prioritize."

Ptol offers a firm nod and leaves with his maintenance bag. Xool sighs, adjusts his glasses, and stares at the obelisk. He furrows his eyebrows and says, "Sir?"

Rosek turns to him, but says nothing.

"I, um, have a question regarding the log."

Rosek remains silent.

Xool shrugs and says, "There were five people on the team?"

"Yes."

"And five before? On the other team?"

"Yes."

"In the mission file," Xool says and flips through a stack of papers, "it says there are twelve missing."

"The original pioneers," Rosek says. "They discovered the Grakinium and its frequency properties."

Xool shrugs and says, "Then, wouldn't they *know* if the Grakinium was radioactive?"

"Yes."

Xool pouts his lips in thought. "Then you don't believe it's radiation poisoning?"

"If I'm here," Rosek says, "then it's not."

Outpost Mission 883
Entry 14: Travel Expenses

Yalena exits her room while everyone else is still asleep. Wearing a simple, travel bodysuit with basic armor, Yalena makes her way down to the kitchen on the second floor. After exiting the narrow stairwell, the automatic lights in the kitchen turn on, and Yalena halts in place to see Rosek standing at the far end of the kitchen.

Yalena attempts to control her breathing as her heart rate spikes and she casually moves to the refrigerator in her black bodysuit with silvery armor pieces over her joints and main muscle groups.

In the shadows of the kitchen, Rosek lowers the half-bitten apple from his helmet and shuts the visor before he walks out into the lit area. He watches her daintily rummage, if a lady of her type could muster a rummage, and she finally discovers something worth a full pinch of pressure from her fingers. She pulls out a sealed meat slice from a stack, shuts the fridge, and throws the packaged food into a heating unit by the fridge. After slapping the door shut, she enters a few commands and watches the machine light up when in use. The packaging wriggles, melts into the steak, and when the machine is done cooking the meat steams with juicy flavor.

Yalena grabs a plate from one of the drawers, slaps it on the table, and then slaps the steak onto the plate. She snags eating utensils from another drawer and pulls out the stool to sit and stare at her midnight dinner.

Across the kitchen island, Rosek remains still and inert. Yalena slowly stares up at him, folds her napkin across her lap, and says, "What, Commander?"

"Meat at night causes nightmares."

Yalena briefly raises one eyebrow and casts her eyes down to her food. She starts to cut the meat with a sharp knife and says, "It's a welcoming sensation."

"The nightmares or the meat?"

Yalena drops her knife and fork. She sighs through her nose and stares at him. "Am I under your personal investigation, Commander?"

"Yes."

Yalena slowly picks up her eating utensils and resumes eating. She swallows a few bites before she says, "I may be a Cold Rib, but I am not a killer like you."

"Like me?"

"Yes," Yalena says and cuts another piece. "When I cut people…they are already dead."

"A family profession."

"Yes. My father, his father, and so on," Yalena says. "No one bothers me in my profession, perhaps because I resemble the dead myself, and in that way I may be considered a mental threat to the stability of this team. I assure you, Commander, that my mind is sound, stable, and I would be more concerned with Dr. Nekang's overwhelming symptoms of megalomania."

Rosek slowly folds his arms. "Your father's cause of death says otherwise."

Yalena eats a piece of meat, swallows, and stares at Rosek. "The profession ate at his mind after my mother passed away. He stopped using protective face filters and succumbed to Toxic Cadaver Syndrome. While I slept, he tried to perform an autopsy on me. I had no choice but to defend myself at the age of sixteen."

Rosek unfolds his arms.

Yalena cuts another piece of meat. "When your own Cold Rib father cannot recognize you as a living person, then, yes, things like depression do seep into a person's soul. Among...other feelings."

Rosek remains silent.

"When I work," Yalena says and stares at Rosek through her long, black lashes. "I know there is at least one difference between me and the dead. They are on the table. I am not."

Rosek watches her continue to eat. He holds up his half-eaten apple and appears to study it. He turns to Yalena and says, "Two, actually."

Yalena stops eating and stares at him.

"You," Rosek says and walks to the stairwell, "still have a soul. Goodnight."

Yalena waits until he is gone before she drops her fork and stops eating. She leans her head into her hand as her elbow props on the kitchen island. She silently cries as the lights turn off and she stays down in the dark until she can sense the others moving around above her.

Ptol turns a hyper-wrench to the side as the bite still clings to the horizontal pipe. He tightens the angle of the wrench head and pushes down until the pipe sealant turns white at the seam of the two pipes. He sits half in a jungle of pipes while his legs flicker with artificial lightning from the main hallway. With a grunt, Ptol releases the wrench and throws it into his bag while he grabs another tool.

Outside the maintenance hatch, a pair of skinny legs wrapped in an orange raincoat stop by the edge of Ptol's tool bag.

"Hey, kid," Ptol says. "Can you grab the black tape?"

"Oh, uh, sure thing!"

Ptol hears Xool rooting around in the tool bag. After a few seconds, a small roll of pipe tape hits Ptol in the shoulder and rolls down into a pile of immediate tools. Ptol smirks and says, "Thanks. How long before we reach the planet?"

"About three weeks."

"Oh great," Ptol says and shakes his head as he uses a pair of clamps on a leaking pipe. "Three weeks of this is going to turn me into a soggy grump."

"Huh? Why?"

"Somebody keeps using the hot water on max," Ptol says. "It's testing these recycled pipes and nobody's been maintaining them since…uh, looks like never."

"Yikes."

"Yeap," Ptol says and shoves a long, wooden stick between his sharp teeth. "I'm guessing the dead girl."

Xool's eyes widen and he nervously looks around. "Hey, uh, not so loud!"

"I'm not scared of that high-heeled prude."

"She can't help it."

"This is going on my report as extra! I'm no plumber."

"Hey uh, you want some coffee or something?"

Ptol stops tightening a pipe. "Huh?"

"You want, like, something to warm you—"

"I heard you," Ptol says and sighs as he wipes grease off his face. He grumbles and says, "Sure, if it's not—"

"Be right back!"

Ptol hears Xool running off to the nearest stairwell. He shrugs and returns to working. After a few minutes, Ptol perks his ears and grimaces at the maintenance hatch.

"I know you're there," Ptol says. "I don't like it when people sneak up on me."

Rosek's boots step into view. "This is not your occupation, Mech Master Ptol."

Ptol chuckles as he tightens a bolt. "You're not wrong, but I don't know anyone else on board who can keep the hot water pipes from bursting, let alone the tools. You going to shoot the plumber?"

"Not yet."

Ptol laughs and says, "Ha! If that's your way of accusing me of sabotage…you better check your six at night, fish boy."

"You sabotaged one ship before."

Ptol frowns and stops working. "Allegedly."

"Prove me wrong."

"Ha! You're all the same," Ptol says and pulls himself out of the hatch. He stands up and stares directly into Rosek's helmet visor. "If you read the incident report, then you'd know I was *ordered* to reset the airlock systems because they were malfunctioning. It's not my fault the dumb captain thought that would fix the issue while I was taking a break."

"You knew resetting them wouldn't fix them?"

"Well, yeah. There were other issues I had to resolve before I could professionally deem them safe. The co-captain was just covering his backend by accusing me. The fact he became the new captain...hey, why don't you investigate that? I lost my job and he got a promotion. Isn't that great? Now, get out of my business!"

Rosek merely takes one step back as Ptol opens his mouth and roars. His muscles jack up as a tail swishes behind him. After a few seconds, Ptol calms down and returns to fixing the hot water pipes.

Down in the kitchen, Xool makes a pot of coffee from the jug-sized apparatus. Arch Legathes sits on the bench and stares out the window into space behind him as Dr. Nekang reads a book at the kitchen island.

Glancing to Xool, Nekang smirks and says, "Pulling coffee duty?"

"I like being nice," Xool says. "Whatever helps the team, I'm all for it."

Nekang quietly shuts his book. "How many missions have you completed, Xool?"

"Oh, uh," Xool says and smiles. "This is my first one."

Legathes smiles.

"Well," Nekang says and walks over to him. "Don't be surprised if people don't share your optimistic approach."

Xool points at him and smiles. "Hey, double negative."

Nekang frowns and grabs a cup. As he searches for sugar, he sighs and says, "I'm not sure you're built for this line of work, Xool. You see, we are all experts in our respective fields and, not to offend you, you seem straight out of nav training."

Xool laughs nervously and adjusts his glasses. "Well, no offense taken, but I passed all my map tests ten years ago."

"Really? So young?"

"Psh," Xool says and grabs a thermos. He pours fresh, hot coffee into the thermos and shuts the cap. He shrugs and says, "I'm sorry you were so old when you finished."

Legathes refrains from laughter as Xool skips up the stairwell and Dr. Nekang grumbles to himself. He pours a large cup of coffee and glances to Legathes.

"You are also young," Nekang says. "This is a highly classified mission. You and Xool do not have enough experience to be trusted with such sensitive information."

Legathes turns around and stares at Nekang. "How young do you think I am, doctor?"

"You look the same in years to Xool."

"I appreciate that," Legathes says and stands. "I am closer in age to Rosek than I am to you and Xool."

Nekang blinks and says, "You're Hynibrian, correct?"

"Yes."

"I thought," Nekang says and takes a sip of coffee, "that the Hynibrians were myths and lived average lifespans."

Legathes smiles and walks over to the coffee maker. He grabs a cup, but then he pours water from the fridge into his cup. He walks past Nekang and says, "My aging process is average compared to other Hynibrians, but not to other lifeforms. There is good reason why my people were hunted by the Zeniths...and it was not for our healing abilities or faith. They could not achieve that by opening up our bones. Faith is acquired through belief, not bloodletting."

"So it's true," Nekang says. "Your people believe that your faith keeps you young."

Legathes softly puts his hand over his chest and offers a slight bow. He straightens and leaves.

Nekang takes another sip of coffee as his tight gloves twist. "A man who does not indulge in small doses of harmless coffee cannot be trusted."

As Nekang talks to himself, Legathes walks up to the first floor where Xool waits for him. Xool smiles and says, "I thought you were my age."

"I am sorry to disappoint you," Legathes says. "Surely your gift to map and travel is from a higher power."

Xool shrugs and says, "That would be nice."

"Do you not believe this?"

"I'm still figuring things out," Xool says as they walk down the hall. "I'm not saying no, but I am saying I don't know."

Legathes smiles. "That is better than most."

"Did the Zeniths catch you? Did you escape like Rosek?"

"I was away on another mission," Legathes says, "when the Zeniths attacked my world. When I returned, I saved many of my people from starvation and death. My faith kept me safe so that I could help my people."

"Zeniths make me nervous," Xool says. "Do you do anything weird? You know, like levitate or something?"

"No, not at all," Legathes says. "I only heal."

"Right," Xool says. "Where's your medical bag?"

"I do not need one."

"The ship's medical bay has everything."

"I do not need that either."

"How do you fix people, then?"

"You will see," Legathes says and walks down another hallway. Xool walks towards the last place he saw Ptol, but he nearly slams into Rosek's chest armor.

"Oh! Sorry, boss!"

"What is that?"

Xool looks at the thermos. "Uh, coffee?"

"For you?"

"No," Xool says and his eyes dart about. "For Ptol."

"That is not your occupation."

"Yeah, well," Xool says and shrugs. "Wouldn't it be cool if they had waitresses in the budget on these long flights? I'm always hopeful."

"Yeah?"

"Yes," Xool says and laughs to himself. "I heard that, on those really big missions, they have attendants. Is it true? Do they wear…little, skimpy uniforms?"

Rosek sighs through his helmet. "Keep dreaming."

Xool smiles as Rosek walks past him and down the same hallway Legathes took. Sprinting over to Ptol's legs,

Xool extends the thermos into the maintenance hatch. Ptol drops his tools, pulls himself out, and unscrews the thermos cap. He takes a sip and makes a great sigh with a grin.

"Oh yeap," Ptol says. "That's strong! Just what I needed. You're the best."

"I didn't know how much to use. I don't drink coffee."

"It'll knock the hair off my feet," Ptol says and takes another sip. "Well, for a few days."

Xool glances to Ptols worn, black boots with oversized toe sections. He blinks and says, "Wait, you're a Gurrusho, aren't you?"

"Yeap," Ptol says and taps his nose. "I can smell you before I see you, kid. I knew you were coming with a hot and steamy five-scooper."

"Whoa! That's impressive!"

"How'd you get stuck on this mission, anyways?"

"Well, there was a spot open," Xool says and shrugs. "I mean, it was open forever, so I figured I should help."

"The pay didn't convince you?"

"Sure it did," Xool says, "but I mainly just like meeting new people. I like to travel."

"Travel these days is dangerous," Ptol says and takes a big swig. "Zeniths aren't the only problems we have. I'm sure you've heard about those Enidrome traffickers. Some say the Enidromes sell people to the Zeniths. My cousin almost got taken by an Enidrome, but his nose saved him."

"Why is that?"

"Enidromes smell like rotten fish," Ptol says and taps Xool on the temple with a clawed finger. "Remember that."

Xool rapidly nods as Ptol crawls back into the hatch. Rubbing the back of his neck, Xool yawns and says, "I have to get back to the nav. Need anything?"

"Nah," Ptol says. "I'm perfect, kid. Go get to work."

Xool nods and jogs to the navigation deck. As he enters the room, he sees Rosek studying the Mater Ves planetary terrain. Most of the terrain is blurry, which means information is not available, and Rosek zooms in on certain rock formations while he takes notes inside a paper journal.

"You know, sir," Xool says as he walks over to his work station. "I'm sure I can find you a wrist snap to log all of your notes inside instead of that fragile book."

"I like paper," Rosek says. "Good for memory."

"Oh," Xool says and shrugs. "Don't trust anything with a frequency?"

"No."

"Yeah, I understand," Xool says and laughs to himself as he studies the route. "Hey uh, Commander? I have a question. How come there's breathable air on Mater Ves if the planet is entirely Grakinium?"

Rosek stops writing.

"I mean," Xool says and adjusts his glasses. He enters a few commands to shorten the route by a day and says, "was there a former colony? If there was, it's not in the mission database or Outpost Archives. I was curious to look before accepting the mission."

Rosek slightly turns his helmet to Xool.

"There's no terraforming equipment, otherwise one of the surveyors would have a specialty in equipment repair, you know, like Ptol. I just think it's strange."

While Xool continues to attempt shortening the route, Rosek returns to taking notes. There is a place where he has zoomed in on the planet, nearly one hundred feet above the surface, and a deserted campsite is visible. Cargo boxes are strewn about, tents are thrashed to pieces, and not a body in sight.

In the observatory room, Yalena drinks something out of a silver canister as she stares out at space. Sitting on a smooth, long bench, Yalena wears a solemn expression as her blonde hair falls down her shoulders in messy waves. She continually presses her lips together, to rush blood into them, and the red pout that appears is almost mesmerizing against her pale, grey skin. The dark circles under her eyes remove the life from her, make her appear like a socketed skeleton ready for burial, and her red lips only look like a final gesture of adoration before she is lowered into the ground.

Arch Legathes strolls into the room, glances to her, and quickly slows to a halt. He turns halfway to her, watches her take another sip from her canister, and sighs.

Yalena stares up at him in the observatory reflection. She swallows and says, "What?"

"You are in great pain," Legathes says. "May I be of any assistance?"

Yalena shoves her canister away in her black bag. "No."

Legathes smiles. "I can fix it."

Yalena blinks and says, "No you can't. The damage is done. I'm not getting any more surgery."

"I don't do that," Legathes says and carefully sits beside her. "All I require is your trust."

Yalena makes a short laugh. She shakes her head and says, "The last person I trusted...tried to kill me."

"I am sorry, Yalena."

"I see why others don't like you," Yalena says and looks at him. "You know things without any information."

Legathes offers a sad smile. "My source is much higher than an archive or database. Your soul never rests with the constant, physical injuries inflicted upon you at a young age. Please, allow me just one chance to show you I can fix them, Yalena."

Yalena swallows, looks away from him, and grips her own right arm sleeve. "No."

Legathes smiles and says, "Can't you trust me? I can fix you, Yalena."

Yalena reaches in her bag, stands, throws the canister on the floor, and says, "It was the last of my painkiller, anyways."

"You don't need it," Legathes says. "Please? Don't drink that poison anymore."

Yalena briskly takes her leave as Legathes stares at the canister. After a few moments of silence, he stands, picks up the canister, and throws it away in a wall disposal unit. He stares at his hands, the filth of poison coating them like a wax seal, and he rubs his hands to feel his fingerprints again. He stares out into the waters, the distant and cold stars, and he listens to the canister as it tinkers down into the bowels of the ship and incinerates.

Outpost Mission 883
Entry 19: Chain of Command

Hovering in orbit over a planet covered in swirling blue storm clouds, the *Manifest* remains silent as all crew members stand and stare out the navigation deck windows. Nested within a crimson gas field, Mater Ves seems to pulsate and sync with the air system rattles while flashes of golden thunder split across the multiple storm eyes like the veins in a bloodshot eye.

Rosek's helmet hisses as he exhales and he whips about to Xool. Taking only two paces towards him, Rosek folds his arms and says, "When will the storms stop?"

"Not sure," Xool says and checks his trajectory map. "Says the planet is clear. It's not registering what we're seeing."

"That's not possible."

"I understand," Xool says, fixes his glasses, and quickly runs a few models. "According to our element log, it's heavy winds and *lots* of Grakinium."

Yalena smiles. "It's a dust storm."

Dr. Nekang adjusts his shirt and peers out the window. "A Grakinium dust storm? We'll certainly have zero visibility of the surveyor site."

Ptol scratches his chin and says, "Yeap. Grakinium in that amount will disrupt the navigations and quite possibly the central systems. We'll have to wait until the storm settles."

Legathes remains silent.

"Unable to comply with request," Rosek says and turns to the crew. "You are not in charge of this mission, Ptol."

Ptol holds up his clawed hands. "Never said I was."

"Hold on," Xool says and shoves an ear device into his almost orange right ear. "I'm picking up something!"

Ptol stomps over to the communications dash next to the driver's seat. He punches in a few commands and starts twisting one of the frequencies.

"C-come in," someone says. "Do not land. I repeat. Do…not…land."

Yalena and Legathes exchange glances.

"Hey," Xool says. "That sounds like the girl from the visual log file!"

"C-come in," someone says over the scattered frequency. "I'm…running out of time. Please, it all starts over. I need time…do not land. The others…are dead. They ran out of time. Time…do not land."

The communicator shuts off.

"Well," Ptol says and turns to Rosek. "I'm not saying I'm in charge, but maybe we shouldn't land?"

"Could be a trick," Dr. Nekang says. "I've heard the Zeniths will play that reverse psychology nonsense. The other teams might be gone, even dead like the distress beacon says, and it could be just a collection of sounds from that one girl on the log file."

Yalena furrows her eyebrows and says, "If the Zeniths found the Grakinium…"

Xool swallows and says, "Bad day for everyone."

Ptol snorts and says, "Nah. Zeniths give off a particular scent. They're a mixture of engine grease and blood scabs. The air would be swimming in it."

Rosek slowly turns his head to Ptol. "Is it?"

"Nah," Ptol says and sniffs. "The air intake pulls oxygen from the surrounding space molecules. I'd smell it since yesterday when we arrived."

Yalena waves a hand up in surrender. "We are not prepared to handle a Zenith encounter. Are we?"

"Yes," Rosek says and walks up to the driver's seat. "I have the necessary weaponry to dispel a small Zenith hunting unit."

"Not a mothership," Dr. Nekang says and points at the planet. "They might be using the planet as a forwarding base. We don't know! How can this much Grakinium go unnoticed? It's highly suspicious."

"To the best of our knowledge," Rosek says. "We are the only ones who know. If the Zeniths discovered it, they did so in-between our survey teams and took them hostage. I have no choice but to enact rescue protocols."

Yalena purses her lips. "Rescue protocols? That wasn't in the job description."

"Not yours," Rosek says. "Mine."

Legathes steps forward. "I will assist you in any way possible, Commander."

"Noted," Rosek says and turns to the others. "According to Outpost laws, we must attempt rescue and recovery. Gathering intelligence on missing teams is a priority. We will also have to gather core samples."

Dr. Nekang nods and says, "I'll get my coring gear."

Xool watches Dr. Nekang leave the room.

Rosek turns to Yalena. "If we find any bodies, Enidrome or otherwise, you must determine cause of death, especially if it has any probability of being Zenith origin."

Yalena swallows and says, "If it is Zenith?"

Rosek nods and says, "Then we depart immediately."

The ground is ash grey, cracked like dry mud, and not a single tree dots the barren landscape. A blink of blue hits the pastel grey skies and the *Manifest* zooms closer. With a whirring and expulsion of downward thrust, the ship lands gracefully without error.

Once the ramp slides out from under the side door, Rosek exits the ship in complete stealth, his gear strapped to his back like a shield of guns, and in his hands is a large pulse rifle that delivers fatal doses of hcart-stopping electrical rounds. After securing the perimeter, Rosek signals Ptol out next, who exits with a pulse shotgun, and his clawed feet click down the ramp.

Ptol stands beside Rosek who continues to look through his rifle scope. He perks his long, wolf-like ears and says, "I don't hear anything. Might have stealth gear."

"Yeah," Rosek says and scans the area. "Zeniths have that."

"Do they have cloaking devices for their ships, too?"

"Yes."

"Any frequency output? Auras? Electrical distortion?"

"No," Rosek says and scans the area. "Ghosts."

"How did you escape?"

Rosek lowers his gun and turns to Ptol. "I didn't."

Ptol blinks with a nervous expression as Xool, Dr. Nekang, Yalena, and Legathes exit the ship. Dr. Nekang and Yalena are wearing the radiation suits as they test the air with equipment. Xool appears hesitant, adjusts his glasses, and tightens his flak jacket. Legathes does not wear any body armor or tactical gear and he simply puts a hand on Xool's shoulder to calm him.

"Oh yeah," Ptol says and lowers his gun. "Forgot about that. I don't smell any radiation."

"He's right," Yalena says and unzips her suit. She steps out in her tactical body suit and sees Rosek turn towards her. She straightens and says, "Negative for radiation."

Dr. Nekang reluctantly removes his suit and adjusts his leathery gloves with a smug expression.

Xool lifts his arm and starts scanning the area with his wrist band map. He spins about and points south. "The surveyor camp is this way. Yalena? I'm showing still bodies…"

Yalena stomps over to Xool as Dr. Nekang peers over Xool's shoulder at the map. Yalena yanks Xool's arm, studies the map, and says, "Three bodies. Obvious struggle. I need to inspect them quickly."

Rosek nods and moves ahead of them. He signals Ptol to take flank. He points at Legathes and says, "Stay directly behind me. The rest of you hang behind him. Ptol, you and I move ahead. Let's go."

Once the ship seals shut and cloaks, Rosek moves the team south. As they travel, the landscape remains the same in all directions.

Xool continues to inspect the map and walks close to Legathes. He presses his lips thin and says, "Strange planet. It's completely flat."

Legathes perks his long ears. "What do you mean?"

"No mountains, canyons, volcanoes…nothing to indicate tectonic plates or even continental shifts. It almost seems…no, that can't be right."

Legathes leans his head to the side. "What?"

"It's," Xool says and shakes his head. "Designed."

Legathes smiles. "All planets were designed."

"Yeah, uh, but *this* planet doesn't have those qualities. It's man-made."

Rosek halts the group. Everyone stops talking. They watch Rosek check through his rifle scope, signal them to stay, and he sweeps forward in silence. Ptol guards the front of the group while Rosek enters the decimated surveyor camp.

Stepping over a broken tent pole, Rosek sneaks his way around to make sure the place is secure. Tent flaps hang dead in the windless air, pots and pans lie strewn about, and Rosek finally reaches one of the dead bodies.

Halfway taken under the ground, the horrific expression on the half-decomposed face tells Rosek this man was taken by complete surprise. A huge hole gapes in the back of his skull, another in his chest, and his fingers are missing. The other two bodies are close to each other, gripping in fear, and the lower halves of their bodies are also buried.

Suddenly, Rosek lifts his gun and swings back around to see the entire team behind him. He growls, lowers his gun, and says, "I told you to wait!"

Yalena stomps up to him with her black bag. "For your own safety, Commander, I'll need to inspect the bodies for potential pathogens."

Rosek remains still as she shoves by him and kneels next to the dead surveyor. He listens to her bag click open, the latex gloves stretch about her long fingers, and the safety mask she puts over her face completes the zombie coroner ensemble. Slowly turning to watch her work, the rest of the team hides behind Rosek, and Rosek observes a tiny pair of tweezers in her gloved fingers.

Yalena plucks at the surveyor's clothing, takes note of the starchiness, and she recovers his badge. *Utorwe, Surveyor Division 3, Lead Surveyor.*

"It's the Lead Surveyor," Yalena says. "Captain Utorwe of the second surveyor team."

Rosek rolls his shoulders. "Anything else?"

Yalena pouts her lips and lifts her mask. She stands, starts removing her gloves, and says, "This man was attacked from behind. Head wound was first, then chest wound."

Dr. Nekang snorts and says, "How could you possibly know that?"

Yalena glares at him. "The wounds were made by different weapons. The first one was from a distance, possibly a rifle, and the second wound in the chest was made up close. His heart was removed with a claw-like device. This man has been dead since the day of the log file. They were attacked either that same night or moments after the log."

Rosek walks up to Yalena and says, "Zenith?"

"No," Yalena says. "These wounds are consistent with Enidrome organ trafficking."

The entire group groans.

Rosek silences them and returns his focus to Yalena. "Are you positive?"

Yalena nods.

Rosek turns to Ptol. "You're a Gurrusho."

Ptol presses his lips thin. "Yeap."

"Can't smell them?"

"Nah," Ptol says and stares at the corpse. "They're getting smarter. They never touched him. I can't smell any trace of them."

Yalena leans close to Rosek. "Perhaps the dust storm removed all traces?"

"That is possible," Rosek says. "Either way, if there are Enidromes here…we are still missing two from the second team, five from the first, and the original two pioneers. Please inspect the remaining two bodies to confirm, Yalena."

Yalena nods and grabs her bag. As she walks over to the other bodies, Rosek circles the group and inspects their expressions.

"This is now a rescue mission," Rosek says. "To prevent further loss of life, you will not return to the ship. You will stay with me until I can locate the Enidrome encampment. They most likely already know we are here, so we do not have much time."

Dr. Nekang frowns and says, "Why can't we go back to the ship?"

Rosek snaps his head to Dr. Nekang. "I don't want any of you getting ideas about marooning the rest of us. If the Enidromes find the ship, we can't get home."

Ptol raises his free hand. "Sir, what about the surveyor ships? I can run a scan for them using their beat up equipment I saw in that tent over there."

"Do it."

Ptol slings his shotgun onto his back and jogs into one of the large, broken tents. Xool joins him. Legathes kneels beside the dead surveyor and frowns as Dr. Nekang joins Ptol and Xool.

Rosek turns to Legathes.

"If he was struck at a distance," Legathes says and looks at Rosek, "why is his face this way?"

"I will inquire," Rosek says and walks over to Yalena. He watches her rise from the two bodies, like a Valkyrie on a battlefield, and she tosses her face guard aside like a bad idea. She removes her gloves with such passion that Rosek thinks she might be offended that there are dead people around.

"I heard him," Yalena says. "Judging by their position in the camp, these two died first. Although they may have been struck at the same time at different angles, Captain Utorwe saw these two men die, hence the expression. Their wounds are the same, fatal blow to the head followed by heart removal, but this one's internal organs were also taken."

Rosek remains silent.

Yalena blinks and watches Legathes walk into the tent. She gives Rosek her full attention and says, "For a hardline man like yourself, I never thought I'd hear you say please."

Rosek starts to turn away, pauses, and says, "New habit."

Yalena smiles as he remains on guard. Her smile quickly fades as she stares down at the man with a full extraction workup. The ribs are strewn about, pieces of vertebrae pried off, and even his fingers are gone. Yalena knits her brow, kneels down, and studies the fingerless hand.

"Yalena? What is it?"

"This is strange," Yalena says. "This sort of injury is only made so that the body cannot be identified, but the name badges are still on their suits."

Rosek walks over as he keeps his head on a swivel. "What do you think?"

"Perhaps we should ask Dr. Nekang," Yalena says and stands. "He may know Enidrome behavior better than I."

"How many Enidrome cases have you completed?"

"Hundreds," Yalena says, "but normally there is either no body or only hollow bodies left. Like I said, this is different."

"Understood."

"Commander Rosek," Yalena says. "Do you know anything about this? Have you seen it before?"

"Negative," Rosek says. "Why?"

"You once wondered if you could trust me," Yalena says and walks up to him. "How can I trust you?"

Rosek fully turns towards her. "Your current position in the team does not require trust, only compliance."

Yalena raises her eyebrows. "I may be a Cold Rib, Commander, but I do believe you are colder."

Rosek watches her walk to the tent and disappear inside. Within seconds he is gone, makes his rounds to secure the perimeter, and in the distance he hears the howl of dust storms ready to roll across the flatlands. Waves of total blackout. Blankets of fatal visibility. With what little time he has, Rosek removes poles from the broken tents to secure them back to the main tent. Legathes assists him, but soon they must all take cover inside the tent as black and blue clouds of Grakinium cover the known area.

Outpost Mission 883
Entry 25: Alternative Means of Transportation

Golden thunder spreads along the rolling black clouds that cover the known visual flatlands. Like the underbelly of crashing waves against a stormy shore, the clouds swirl into one another, twisting and sparkling eddies, and the team is confined to the safety of the surveyor tent.

Most of them sit in a circle around the small self-powered heater, but Yalena stands off and to the back as if she is ready to suddenly flee out from under a sudden attack. The entire group snaps heads towards the entrance, Ptol ready with his shotgun, and Rosek walks in as he brushes piles of metallic black glitter from his shoulders.

Keeping his gun in his right hand, Rosek waits for Ptol to lower his gun before he moves any closer to the group.

Xool adjusts his glasses. "Anything, Commander?"

"Whatever tracks there were," Rosek says, "they are now gone."

"Shame," Ptol says and slowly sits. "Care for something to eat? I just made everyone some canned slop with coffee."

"No," Rosek says. "Hunger keeps me focused."

Yalena frowns and says, "Anything to drink, Ptol?"

Ptol smirks and says, "Ha, I'm not sharing my stash."

Yalena slouches and watches Rosek continually look outside the tent flap. She steps forward and says, "Based on the bodies, there are at least four Enidromes."

Dr. Nekang nods and says, "They usually travel in hunting groups of that size. They call them clutches, not squads."

Rosek sighs through his helmet. "The bodies are gone."

The entire group leaps up.

Yalena blinks and says, "Gone?! When?"

"During my patrol," Rosek says. "No tracks."

Yalena jogs up to Rosek. "Take me to one! Quickly!"

Rosek nods as Yalena puts on her face guard. She takes hold of his left forearm as he barrels out into the storm with his gun ready. In several seconds, they are at the other end of the camp where the bodies were found. As Yalena kneels down, she touches the concave ground with her medical-gloved hands and digs.

Rosek's helmet tips to the side as he watches her dig about. The howling winds are nearly deafening, but he manages to pick up her scratching and pawing. Suddenly, Yalena yelps, Rosek's instinct is to grab the collar of her shirt and yank her behind him, and he nearly falls into a gaping hole in the ground. Yalena clutches him as he peers down into the bottomless hole.

Turning on the light at the end of his rifle, Rosek kneels by the edge and inspects the hole. He jerks back once he sees an entirely underground chasm, hollow and endless, and his light never touches the sides or bottom. He can see underground mountains in the distance, where the light twinkles through the thinner areas, and he can even see building structures even further away.

Yalena almost looks, but suddenly Rosek pushes her back as he retreats from the hole. He grabs her wrist and yanks her back towards the camp tent. Without a second thought, Rosek slams into the tent, signals everyone to move out, and they scramble with immediate panic.

Arch Legathes slowly rises, his expression one of concern, and he is the first to leap from the tent with Rosek and Yalena as he uses his hood to cover his face. The others follow Ptol out, who can smell the front of the group without much visual need, and they move south at an alarming rate.

"Rosek," Yalena says as she tries to pry his iron grip off of her wrist. "What did you see?"

Rosek shakes his head and breaks into a jog. The others struggle to keep his pace, but eventually they exit the Grakinium clouds and into the dark flatlands. Stars light their way in the pale blue scenery as Xool wheezes to catch his breath.

"Commander," Legathes says as he walks over to Xool. "They are not military personnel. They cannot be pushed in this manner."

"They either push," Rosek says and finally releases Yalena. She rubs her wrist as Rosek walks up to Legathes and says, "Or we all die. This planet is hostile."

Everyone gasps.

"What are you saying," Dr. Nekang says. "There is no record of any civilization on this planet."

"I saw a city," Rosek says, "buried under a Grakinium dome."

"If they were sealed inside," Nekang says, "it is not possible they would still be alive."

Ptol nods and says, "Then we cancel the mission and head off! Let's get out of here!"

Rosek turns his helmet to Ptol. "You don't understand, do you?"

Yalena sighs and closes her eyes. "The surveyor ships are gone, but maybe the Enidromes confiscated them."

Xool shakes his head as he looks at his wrist band map. "I'm not seeing the ship anymore. Oh no! We're stranded?!"

Everyone starts to panic.

"Stop," Rosek says and silences them. "Our mission stands as is. Locate the remaining surveyor crew, dead or alive, and find a way off of the planet."

Xool makes a nervous laugh and says, "We don't have a beacon! We have no way of communicating distress!"

"I have one," Rosek says and taps one of the pockets on his tactical vest. "We are not in distress as of now. We must keep moving so the enemy does not fixate on our location."

Ptol shrugs and says, "Who? The Enidromes? What now?"

"Xool," Rosek says. "Run a scan for biological life."

"Uh," Xool says and turns pale. "I...don't really—"

"Now!"

"Yeah, sure!"

Everyone watches Xool tap away on his band until it beeps twice. He shudders and points east. "Uh, there are eight lifeforms in that direction."

"Eight?"

"Y-yes, sir," Xool says and swallows, "I mean, it appears to be eight. I can't make much out of the interference."

Rosek stomps over and grabs Xool's wrist. Xool yelps as Rosek twists his arm to view the image. The entire screen shows signs of life all around, but the warmest bodies are eight figures to the east. He growls to see four are definitely Enidrome figures.

"Enidromes," Rosek says. "The others must be the surveyors. Follow me and no talking."

A flat and sickly green ship sits in the baking sun. From underneath slides a long, black ramp where two massive bodies stand with guns. Their armored bodies require no space suits, built like muscled crabs with spiky joints, and their faces are horrific. Four twitching and clawed fingers sprout off the sides of their ear-to-ear jaws filled with sharp, inward curved teeth. Atop their armored heads are fidgeting antennae that squeak and grind with cockroach disgust. Their eyes are dull and black, rolling in their skulls like vermin chameleon hybrids, and when they speak dribbles of black goo pour down their armored chests and torsos.

One walks out with silver pins pushed into his shoulders and barks at the other two who quickly stand straighter and run inside. He spits on the ground, walks back inside, and the ramp closes.

As he walks through the wet and mold-ridden halls, someone screams from the prisoner quarters. He laughs, punches his fist into the prison door, and keeps walking. He enters a foul room covered in blood and old skin all over the floor. On the rusting table is a dead surveyor as one Enidrome stands over him with a lab coat and a pair of loppers in his mangled hand.

The leader barks at him, the Enidrome nods, and holds up the hand of the dead surveyor. He lops off the fingers, inspects the wounds, and replies to the leader. The leader nods, studies the fingers, and picks one up to eat it. He shrugs, says a few commands to the butcher, and leaves.

Outside, just within the haze of mirages, Rosek flattens himself along the ground while the others lie flat on either side of him. He is silent for a long time as he looks through his scope.

Yalena slowly crawls up to his left side and says, "Rosek?"

"Confirmed," Rosek says. "Four man hunting party. Someone told them we'd be here."

Yalena's eyes dart about. "W-what?"

"Coverup," Rosek says. "Something bad happened on this rock."

"The Outpost?"

"Improbable. The head of the Outpost personally requested me on this mission. If they wanted it buried, they wouldn't have hired me."

"Then who?"

Rosek slowly lowers his gun and turns to Yalena. "Everyone is a suspect."

Yalena frowns. "Including me?"

"Especially you."

Yalena finally shows signs of emotion and widens her eyes. "You're joking, yes?"

"I am unable to comply."

"What are you? A robot? I went out there with you to investigate the bodies!"

"Does a murderer return to the crime scene, Yalena?"

"What idiot would I be to endanger myself on this planet? I full-heartedly believe in monsters, Commander. Perhaps your eyes should glance to those who believe in nothing!"

Ptol huffs and scratches his ears. "Could you maybe whisper? I can hear everything."

Xool sighs and says, "I wish I could hear that good."

Dr. Nekang huffs and says, "I am uncomfortable on the ground when you say there are things beneath it, Commander!"

Legathes only smiles.

Rosek snaps his head back to his rifle scope. The Enidrome ship ramp slowly slides out of the ship as two Enidromes walk out to smoke.

"Wait here," Rosek says and stands. His motion is fluid, as if he has done this a thousand times, and standing into sprinting seems easy to do when he does it. He sprints like a machine, his gun held along his side to reduce resistance, and he leans into his own insane momentum.

The Enidromes continue to slobber and spit in their language, coughing up goo as they smoke, and they take no notice of the bullet in black running at them so fast he creates a dust wake behind him.

Leaping into the air, catching the sunlight, the Enidromes finally take note of the flicker as they lift their guns, but a crack already sounds through the air as one Enidrome clutches his chest as he falls over dead. Rosek lands on the ramp, fires once in the chest, once in the head, and he doesn't wait for the Enidrome the gurgle as he rolls down the ramp.

With terrifying speed, Rosek strides two steps, plants inside the ship, and runs down the main hall. The scientist Enidrome steps out to see the commotion, loses his head to three incoming bullets, and Rosek leaps over his crumpled body as he heads for the command center.

The leader climbs out of the cockpit, leaps at Rosek with a hooked knife, and Rosek dodges to the left, delivers five kidney stabs with his own knife, and then he manages to squeeze behind the Enidrome captain as he shoves his knife in the body armor seams.

The *Manifest* crew hears a high-pitched scream jettison from the Enidrome ship, then sudden silence, and moments later, Rosek casually walks down the black ramp and waits for them with a single wave to come over.

Arch Legathes immediately stands and sprints to the ship as Yalena and Ptol follow. Xool and Dr. Nekang have a hard time catching up, but Rosek waits for all of them to arrive. Legathes attempts to pass by Rosek, but Rosek firmly grips his shoulder.

"Not yet," Rosek says. "I must clear the ship."

Legathes frowns and says, "I can sense someone is hurt aboard. Let me go!"

"No," Rosek says. "If this is our only way off the planet, I need to clear it…thoroughly. Your patient can wait."

"Patient," Xool says and shrugs. "There were three other survivors…"

Rosek halts at the top of the ramp. "Not anymore."

Once Rosek returns, Legathes sprints inside directly to the prisoner hall. Followed by Yalena and Ptol, Legathes opens one of the doors and nearly gawks in horror. Inside the chamber is what appears to be the remains of a man, partially inside-out, and the rest of him was obviously eaten. They discover a second dead, half-eaten body in another cell nearby.

"Yeap," Ptol says and pinches his nose. "Enidromes ate them up for breakfast."

Legathes backs away and shakes his head. "Monsters!"

Yalena tiptoes around Legathes and starts putting her ear to the other doors in the hallway. Eventually, towards the end, she hears someone sniffing. Yalena gasps and waves to Legathes.

Ptol leaps over, roars, and slams his body into the door until the hinges pop off. After he pries the door off, Legathes and Yalena peer inside to see a woman in an orange surveyor suit chained to the corner.

"No," Legathes says, but Yalena stops him.

"Let me handle this," Yalena says, but the girl looks up at Yalena and screams. Yalena slouches, waves to Legathes, and leaves.

Ptol shakes his head as he watches Yalena trudge down the hallway to the control center.

"It's alright," Legathes says and removes her chains. "You're safe now. My name is Arch Legathes. We are with the Outpost."

The girl tightly shuts her eyes and passes out. Legathes quickly picks up her malnourished body and walks past Ptol.

Following them, Ptol frowns and says, "They were going to eat her last, I guess."

"Why eat the bounty? It does not make sense," Legathes says. He glances about the ship and says, "Their living conditions do not suggest adequate food storage guidelines."

Ptol curls up his nose as his big ears flatten along the sides of his head. He feels the squishy piles of black rot in his boot grooves and says, "Foul! They don't even flush!"

As they walk by the science lab, they pause to see Dr. Nekang and Yalena inside the room. Nekang takes detailed notes in his wrist ledger as Yalena keeps a stern, angry expression.

"Interesting," Nekang says and studies the fingers on the recently deceased corpse. "They are the ones removing fingers...but why?"

Yalena clenches her jaw. "Trophies."

"Perhaps," Nekang says and circles the science table. "I do believe it might be a superstition in their culture. Yes, there was one reference that spoke on this. Some of the older Enidromes come from an outdated culture where they believed spirits could pass through touch, therefore fingers."

Ptol makes a short laugh and keeps walking.

"It is best," Arch Legathes says, "to be wary of their intentions. Do not touch that body. I sense evil from it."

Yalena finally arrives from her distant expression back into her body. She quickly leaves the room, passes by Legathes, and Dr. Nekang greedily eyeballs the available scientific tools in the room.

"I will," Nekang says, "be only a moment."

Legathes frowns and leaves with the surviving surveyor in his arms. He walks all the way up to the command center only to see Ptol vomit on the floor as Rosek births from the cockpit tunnel. Covered in refuse and bowel expulsions, Rosek shakes his shoulders hard and once to remove black slop from his armor. He wipes his helmet clean and turns to Legathes.

"There is a waste purge function," Rosek says. "You all must clear out before activation. Ptol? Have everyone stay back. Bacterial toxicity is a high probability."

Ptol wipes his mouth and offers a weak nod. Legathes stares at Rosek and says, "What about you?"

"The entire ship will fill with churning water," Rosek says. "I am a Tide Man. Stand clear and stay sharp, Legathes."

Legathes watches Rosek brace himself before he dives back into the control center. As he exits the ship to join the others, a loud siren blares aboard the ship while the ramp seals shut. They watch as water seeps out of small crevices along the hull, but soon they realize the water comes from huge tanks on the undersides of the ship. After several minutes, they hear what sounds like a washing machine that then abruptly makes a bang. Great spouts of water shoot out of several gaskets along the sides of the ship, putrid and brown sludge, and Ptol nearly swoons in disgust as he clamps his hands over his nose.

Xool winces at the sight, looks away, and he sees Dr. Nekang slowly putting his gloves back over his hands, but not before he saw Nekang's skinless palms. Xool could see all of the tendons, muscles, and even the veins crawling across the lipid patches. As Nekang glances to him, Xool quickly turns away.

"So gross," Ptol says. "I do *not* want to do the mechanicals in this thing! I'm not getting paid enough for this."

Dr. Nekang smirks and says, "You can comp it."

Ptol shakes his head.

Xool makes a nervous laugh. "Glad I'm the map guy."

"Yeap," Ptol says and grimaces at him. "You have to *slide* into the control center with Rosek, kid."

Xool almost turns green.

Legathes looks down at the unconscious surveyor in his arms. Her eyes move beneath the lids in rapid fire. She twitches in a way that makes him wince, like she's listening to someone being hacked up, and her spine tightens at the end of her nightmare before her eyes shoot open and stare up at him.

She screams, Legathes tries to put her down, and she leaps out of his arms onto the ground. Ptol and Xool leap backwards, Yalena ignores her as she studies her own blue fingernails, and Dr. Nekang stares on with amusement.

"No! No," she says and screams. "I told you to stay away! Now we have to blow up the ship!"

"Whoa there," Ptol says and points at her. "No blowing up! This is our ride off the planet! Legathes, grab her!"

"Calm down, miss," Legathes says and takes a step closer. "You must be Kuressa."

"You don't understand," Kuressa says and shoves her dirty hair out of her face. "When the storms come, we're dead! Everyone is going to die!"

Legathes takes another step closer. "Who killed the other surveyors? The ones at the camp?"

Kuressa shakes her head as she cries. "You can't…"

Dr. Nekang furrows his brow. "Is there a city? Under the ground?"

"It's not ground," Kuressa says and stomps with one foot on the dirt. "It's a cage!"

"A cage for what?"

"It doesn't matter," Legathes says and kneels beside her. "Come with me. You are very tired. I won't let anything happen to you."

Kuressa starts to break down and she collapses to her knees. She cries indistinguishable words as Legathes slowly picks her up. The ship groans as the ramp slides back down. Legathes carries Kuressa back inside the ship. Everyone else goes inside except for Yalena who sits on the edge of the ramp where sunlight can touch her black shoes.

She takes in the heat, hears the Grakinium storm in the north, and holds herself as she stares out into the bleak flatlands. Midday turns into afternoon and still she does not move. Eventually, Yalena senses a presence behind her. She relaxes her shoulders as a shadow drifts across her left side and Rosek sits next to her.

"Will you not go inside?"

"I will not sleep where there are dead people," Yalena says. "Call it…a personal problem."

"I can respect that."

"A body is also missing from Xool's initial count on his band. I'm guessing you are still searching for him."

"You are correct."

Yalena slowly turns to him. "Why are you here?"

"The Outpost hired me to—"

"No," Yalena says and shifts her body towards him. "I know who you are. You're Rosek the Tide Man, the only Zenith survivor from your planet, and somehow you're also a really good assassin and tracker? Don't take me for an idiot, Rosek."

Rosek looks away into the desert. "Hmm."

"You're past doesn't scare me," Yalena says. "You don't even scare me."

"You are the only one who understands," Rosek says. "The only one…I've ever met…that knows."

Yalena offers a rare and sad expression. "You look more alive than I, Commander."

Rosek turns his helmet towards her. "We are dead already, Yalena. Perhaps that gives us an advantage here."

"Why is that? Is there more than just Enidromes?"

"What hunts us," Rosek says and scans the area, "is not detectable. It moves through the earth, like a worm in a coffin, and it eats the living, not the dead. It has a past worse than mine…a present like yours…and there is no time for mercy."

Yalena puts her hand on top of his hand. "What's the plan, then?"

Rosek stands and offers her his hand. "Come with me."

Yalena takes his hand, stands, and they walk inside. The ship no longer smells foul, but there is a lingering rancidness in some corners. Dr. Nekang remains in the science lab, but now he appears to be tidying up a mess of tools all over the floor. The body from the table is gone. Ptol and Legathes work on the medical bay lighting situation while Kuressa carefully huddles in the back inside of a blanket.

Leading her to the control center, Rosek enters first and waits for Yalena to slide inside. She shoots out the other end, but Rosek firmly stands to block her from hitting her head on one of the driving seats. Xool nearly leaps out of his skin as his fingers slime over with clear goop.

"Oh, thank you," Xool says and shudders. "This place creeps me out. Yalena?"

Yalena fixes her slime-covered hair and frowns at Rosek. "This place is gross."

"Xool and Ptol are working on ship diagnostics," Rosek says. "Ptol gave him enough information to get the scanners and maps online. He apparently refuses to enter, so now he's acting as guard for Legathes and you all until the other surveyor turns up."

"I don't blame him."

"Can you drive, Yalena?"

Yalena glances to the steering spike inside of a ball joint. She swallows and says, "It's crude, but I'll manage."

"I only ask because I need you to operate the grappling hook and chain."

Yalena's eyes widen. "What?!"

Xool makes a nervous laugh. "Yeah, I know, right? He wants to go down into the ghost city while Ptol and I repair the ship and run diagnostics before takeoff."

Yalena swiftly turns back to Rosek. "You can't go down there! It's too dangerous."

"I am required to investigate," Rosek says. "If I do not return, I will need you to disembark without me."

Yalena's shoulders slouch. "I won't do it. There's still a missing surveyor. There could be more Enidromes."

"If I am right, you will have no choice."

Rosek removes something from one of his back holsters and hands it to Yalena. She stares into her hands at a gigantic pistol that could knock a man into his grave across the galaxy.

"It's one pulse cartridge, but you can get five shots."

Yalena puts the gun on her hip and folds her arms. "I will operate the chain with only one condition."

Rosek sighs through his helmet. "What?"

"If you can come back," Yalena says. "Do."

Outpost Mission 883
Entry 32: Enemy Territory

Rosek reaches the end of the chain, lands on white dirt, and turns on the light at the end of his rifle. He hears something shuffle behind him, he spins about with his gun up, and only clouds of disturbed dust swirl in the air.

Through Rosek's helmet, he can see in full color day vision. The surrounding area is an old town with halfway buried houses and storefronts. He walks for a mile before his communicator inside his helmet blinks as Yalena's face appears on a small screen to the right.

"Commander," Yalena says. "Ptol is repairing the lift fuel lines for takeoff. We should be able to start diagnostics soon."

"Affirmative," Rosek says and moves forward through the dead city. "Reached ground zero. Investigating city limits. No signs of life."

"Dr. Nekang will not respond to our calls," Yalena says. "Xool did a scan and he's in the lab, but he won't join us up here to explain anything you find down there."

Rosek peers through his rifle scope into the deep city ahead of him. Something big quickly dips down from one of the broken windows. He sighs and says, "I will fear no evil…"

"Rosek?"

"As the forensic pathologist on this team, I might need you more than Dr. Nekang."

"Why?"

Rosek halts and aims his rifle at a nearby building, but all he sees is a dust cloud from inside a fractured doorway. Within the building is a pile of bones, but there is something wrong with them.

They are all mutated and red. Some grow two or three bones out of a single shaft while others grow three joints that hook around in impossible ways. There are no skulls and no spines.

"Sending you visual," Rosek says and sees Yalena's blank expression change into one of confusion.

"Rosek," Yalena says as he continues to move through the environment. "That is extreme radiation overload."

"Yes."

Yalena mutters something to Xool and he runs a few tests. Yalena nods and turns her gaze back to the visual communicator. "Commander, there are no signs of radiation down there, according to your sensors. Can you get closer to one of the piles?"

Rosek spins about suddenly again, but there is only a dust cloud. Xool whines over the communicator. Rosek backs up to the bone pile. "Copy. Inspecting."

"Do not touch them," Yalena says. "It may be a pathogen if there is no radiation. That would explain the containment."

"Containment?"

"Yes," Yalena says. "If this planet held a deadly pathogen, then someone sealed it."

Xool looks up from his work. "Who?"

Rosek stares down at a stray bone and kicks it with his boot. He lingers on the bone as long as he can before a sound spins him about. Another dust cloud.

"That's not pathogenic," Yalena says. "There would be deterioration, but the discoloration would suggest some living presence. Can you—"

Xool yelps as Rosek's helmet whips around, his gun up, and inside the building doorway is a massive shadow. Rosek fires, the light illuminates the monster, and Yalena holds in a scream to see three bodies fused together at the navel that now cartwheel into the building after Rosek.

"Get out of there," Yalena says. "Go!"

Rosek turns off his communicator and blasts the creature into three pieces. The pieces start to move and rejoin, but Rosek does not stay to watch. He runs at full speed, dust nearly catching on fire behind him, and thousands of monsters follow him as they pour out of the city like a tidal wave.

Ptol slides out from a maintenance shaft near the medical bay and stands. He groans, rubs his back, and pauses at the medical bay doorway where Legathes stands. With a glance over Legathes' shoulder, Ptol sees Kuressa still hunkering into the corner.

"Yeap," Ptol says to Legathes. "That's shock."

"She is convinced something is wrong with her team," Legathes says. "I reassured her that we incinerated the discovered remains. My report will put me in an unfavorable light, but I am in agreement with Yalena that there is something wrong with the bodies."

Ptol snorts and says, "I still smell rotting corpses. Are you sure there aren't more in the holding cells?"

"I have already checked twice for you."

"Huh," Ptol says and stomps down the hall. "This whole place stinks of dead people!"

Kuressa shudders at Ptol's raised voice.

Legathes turns to Kuressa and says, "If you trust me, I can help you."

Kuressa shakes her head. "It's coming."

Legathes steps closer to her. "What is?"

In the science lab, Dr. Nekang slowly removes his gloves and stares at his skinned hands. He grimaces, hears Ptol stomping down the hall, and swiftly moves to the doorway.

Ptol walks by the science lab, glances inside, but he does not see Nekang. He sniffs the air, his ears fold back, and he slowly takes out one of his hyper-wrenches.

Ptol steps into the science lab and says, "Dr. Nekang?"

Walking over to the examination table, Ptol sees fresh blood smears that travel down the table and into one of the vents. He growls and walks over to the intercom system. Slamming his fist on the button, Ptol says, "Xool? Hey kid!"

Xool appears on the communicator screen. "What's wrong?!"

"Dr. Nekang is acting weird," Ptol says. "There's a lot of blood in the science lab. I think the loser took my stash out of the fridge. Sorry, Yalena. I was going to share."

"He touched that body," Yalena says as she shoves her way over to the intercom. "He's infected! Xool needs to seal the vents!"

"Kid," Ptol says as he readies his gun. "Go to that far dash with all the slimy red buttons. Those are your latch and bulkhead controls."

Behind Ptol stands Dr. Nekang, but his eyes are bleeding. Xool gasps and says, "Ptol!!"

Yalena and Xool gasp as Ptol screams, the intercom goes black, they hear shots fired, and then there is silence.

Yalena panics, starts smacking Xool on the back, and says, "Shut the vents! Shut them!"

Down the hall from the science lab, Legathes suddenly stands from kneeling beside Kuressa. She also leaps to her feet and hides behind Legathes as gunfire explodes in the science lab.

"Legathes! He's gone mad," Ptol says as he limps into the medical bay. Ptol enters a few commands next to the doorway, the door seals shut, and Dr. Nekang slams his body into the sealed door.

Kuressa screams, Dr. Nekang vomits blood, and Ptol raises his gun at the door.

"No," Legathes says and jogs over to Ptol. "Oh! Your arm! I'll get your leg next."

Ptol lowers his gun and stares at the gaping wound in his right arm. Dropping his gun, Ptol quickly sits on the floor as Legathes grabs hold of his arm.

While Dr. Nekang smears his morphing face along the bloody door, Kuressa redirects her attention to Legathes and his glowing hands. His hands turn almost white as his veins and arteries in his arms glow beneath the skin. Within moments, Ptol's wound seals shut as muscles repair themselves.

"Hold on, friend," Legathes says. "Just another moment."

Kuressa looks at the door as Dr. Nekangs face splits apart to reveal a gory flower filled with teeth. She whines and says, "We don't have a moment."

Dr. Nekang screams, his arms explode off, and two bony ligaments grow in their stead. Clawed, bony hands sprout from the nubs as his guts explode out of his torso. Another head emerges from his torso and then two arms also slide out.

Ptol yelps as the door shatters, he raises his gun, and fires as Legathes finalizes his healing. He blasts Nekang across the room, body parts fly everywhere, and he sighs once everything stops moving.

Legathes immediately stands, Kuressa hides behind him, and Ptol looks up at Legathes.

"Wow," Ptol says, "that was close—"

Legathes grabs Kuressa as Ptol's head suddenly explodes. Ptol's body snaps backwards as ten arms punch through his ribs and back. Legathes sprints from the medical bay with Kuressa and they head for the control center.

Kuressa looks back and screams to see Ptol's body slithering after them with four heads and twenty arms.

Legathes tosses her into the control center tube, turns about, and white light fills the hallway as a terrible scream shakes the walls.

Kuressa screams as she rolls into the control center, Yalena lifts her gun up to avoid shooting her, and Xool taps furiously on the controls.

"I've shut the vents," Xool says. "Running diagnostics!"

Yalena gasps and says, "Where's Legathes?!"

Outside the control center, the light fades and Legathes lowers his glowing white hands. On the ground, Ptol is merely a bubbling pile of black tar. Legathes shudders, perks his ears, and looks up.

Down at the other end of the hall is the missing surveyor and two pioneers. They are bent in terrible ways, the surveyor's head appears to swing from his nonexistent neck, and the pioneers have more than two legs each.

Legathes' eyes widen, they sprint towards him, and Legathes leaps down the control center tube as he screams and says, "Seal the control center! Seal it now!"

As Legathes tumbles into the control center, he hears the passage clamp shut with three bulkheads.

"Whoa," Xool says. "Enidromes are paranoid!"

"That's good news for us," Yalena says and winces as the first bulkhead booms. "Xool! What do we do?"

"Uh, I, uh," Xool says and slides his hands across the wet and grimy control panels. "I don't know!"

Kuressa swallows and says, "They'll find a way in."

Legathes stands and rubs his head. "Can we use the waste purge function?"

"Oh! Right," Xool says and hesitates, "but even this room will fill with water!"

Yalena pleads with Xool. "Can you isolate this room?"

"No," Xool says and shakes his head. "This is an Enidrome ship. They can all breathe underwater. They don't need to...wait..."

The others look at him with hope.

"The holding cells," Xool says and grins. "They are waterproof! Remember? We still had to clear the bodies after the waste purge! If I time the waste purge, we can get inside one of the holding cells!"

Yalena shivers and says, "But there are things out there!"

Legathes nods. "Three. The pioneers and surveyor."

Kuressa covers her face. "They are not people anymore. None of them are..."

Yalena slowly turns her head to Kuressa. "What is it?"

"My team found the dead pioneers," Kuressa says. "They were...halfway pulled into the ground. They all touched them to drag them out and bury them, but I wouldn't do it. I was afraid. Then, overnight, they all started acting crazy. The Enidromes attacked the camp, killed the others, and took me. There were many Enidromes, but then there were only a few. Something was chewing on their fuel lines..."

"We can't linger," Yalena says to Legathes. "These things are smart. We have to purge them now."

Xool nods and says, "I'll set the timer."

Legathes nods and says, "I will make a path. They are evil and do not like my light. Stay close to me."

The group braces themselves as Xool sets the waste purge timer. On the main screen, Enidrome numbers appear in a countdown format, and Xool unlocks the bulkheads. Legathes leaps up into the tube only to face multiple-toothed neck pits screaming at him, and he unleashes a bright light from his hands.

The monsters scream, retreat, and the group follows Legathes out of the tube and down the hall. Sprinting as fast as they can, Yalena scrambles into the nearest holding cell, slams into Legathes, and he shuts the door as Xool and Kuressa pile inside with them.

Just outside the door, the monsters run down the hall past the holding cells. Shivering with fear, Yalena aims her gun at door and tries to keep her arms steady while the countdown continues over the intercom in Enidrome tongue.

"Yalena," Xool says and whispers. "What are you doing?"

"These doors," Yalena says, "open from the outside."

Kuressa huddles in the corner as Xool huddles with her. Legathes raises his palms to the door beside Yalena and says, "If you trust me, I can help."

"We are beyond trust," Yalena says. "It's survival."

Suddenly, the ship alarms go off, they hear water rush in and churn beyond the door as small squirts of water hiss through cracks and holes.

"Oh no," Xool says and whines. "I forgot to set the drain function!"

Legathes frowns and says, "Then we will all drown if this room is compromised."

Kuressa stares at the thin layer of water on the holding cell floor. The water level is slowly rising. She cries and says, "We're going to drown either way."

Suddenly, one of the holding cells creaks and makes a boom. Yalena jerks at the sound, hears the monsters swimming through the holding cell area, and another cell blasts open.

Climbing up the chain, Rosek aims one of his pistols downwards at the horde of distorted creatures attempting to pile on top of one another to reach him. Nearly half a mile up, Rosek can almost reach the edge of the Grakinium ceiling, but then he hears an alarm go off on the ship.

Shooting down again, Rosek watches a five-armed, eight bodied screaming thing with a tube head fall down the monster pile back into the city. The next one rising up has a long neck and no lower jaw on its cracking face.

Rosek holsters his gun, grabs the chain, and climbs up the rest of the way to the surface. Rolling onto the ground, Rosek immediately stands with his rifle in hand, and he runs to the front of the ship. To his shock, the ramp is gone.

He nearly shoots the side door, but then he sees water streams trickling from some of the sealed release valves. He lowers his gun and says, "The waste purge function!"

Rosek abruptly aims his rifle at the hole in the ground, fires twice, and the long-necked monster screams as it falls back down into the ground. Rosek slings his rifle back over his shoulder, sprints, and leaps atop the Enidrome ship. He runs along the top, finds a hatch, and pries it open to see the entire ship is full of water. He takes a few controlled breaths, dives inside, and the hatch seals shut behind him as dozens of creatures pour out of the hole beside the ship.

Swimming through the cloudy hallways, Rosek heads for the holding cells. As he swims, the surveyor twists out of another hallway with hundreds of fingers twitching on his open neck and chest. Rosek takes no time to raise his gun and fire. Ten bullets sent in strategic locations hit the monster in rapid succession. With a cloud of black blood now spilling into the hallway, Rosek panics and swims the other way as the blood seems to move and collect after him. Glancing behind him, Rosek can see the two pioneers swimming after him as well.

Cutting a corner and using his feet to propel off the corner to increase his distance, Rosek heads for the control center. Before he reaches the tube, one of the pioneers grabs his boot.

Rosek flips about, grabs the monster with his gloved hands, and breaks his neck as he kicks him away into the other monster. In a tangle of legs and arms, the monster tries to grab Rosek before he slides down the tube. Rosek enters the control center and initiates drain. A rush of cold water fills the room as jets push water in turbulent, circular motions.

The last monster outside is torn to shreds by the water and the remains are blasted out of the ship onto thousands of living monsters now trying to break through the ship's hull. Rosek sees a blinking light on the panel, slams his fist on it, and the thrusters ignite.

As a huge Grakinium cloud covers the area, golden thunder lights up the monsters from below as Enidrome engine fire burns hundreds of them into less than particles. The ship rips from the horde, enters the sky, and dozens of monsters slide off the sleek, wet ship.

Water continues to spray out of the drain system and Rosek feels his feet float to the ground as gravity returns. He shakes off the soaked feeling, climbs up through the control center tube, and aims his gun down every hall until he reaches the holding cells.

He bangs on one door at a time before he opens them. At the final door, he sees water still pouring out. With a sigh and slouching shoulders, Rosek hesitates with his finger on the release hatch. He bows his head and lowers his hand.

Suddenly, he hears the barrel click on his pulse pistol. One bullet blasts a hole nearly the size of the door as water surges outwards with four halfway drowned bodies. Legathes coughs up water as Xool trips over himself in a sopping mess of panic. Kuressa screams as water pours out of her mouth and Yalena aims the pistol at Rosek.

"Is it you," Yalena says. "Are you contaminated?!"

Rosek hisses a sigh through his helmet. "Affirmative and...negative, Yalena."

Yalena lowers her gun with a heaving sigh. "It's you."

Rosek leans his head to the side. "This is all?"

Legathes stands and says, "There is much to explain."

Xool whines and coughs. "No! Let's just go!"

"We are going," Rosek says. "Gravity stabilizers are activating. We have left the planet's atmosphere."

Yalena wipes her soaked hair out of her face and jerks away as Rosek tries to reclaim his pistol. She shoves on him with a firm hand and says, "No, I'm keeping this until I'm back at my place."

"Whoa," Xool says and elbows her. "That sounded like a—"

Legathes grabs Xool by the ear and leads him towards the control center. "We must run scans, young Xool. Come with us, Kuressa."

Rosek glances to Kuressa who still sits in the holding cell. Her skin is pale and her eyes stare off. He turns his attention back to Yalena.

Yalena presses her red lips thin and says, "Well?"

"I have neutralized all onboard hostiles."

"You want a medal?"

Rosek shifts his weight and says, "You are highly ungrateful."

"If you're expecting a thank you," Yalena says and walks around him. "You'll get it at my place."

Rosek jerks and watches her walk down the hallway towards the control center. He turns his attention back to Kuressa, but she is gone. Rosek searches the area, but he cannot find her.

Walking to the control center, Rosek sees Xool and Legathes exit the tube as Yalena pauses in front of them.

"Xool," Rosek says as he walks towards them. "Locate Kuressa."

Xool shakily points behind Rosek with wide eyes.

Rosek braces himself, spins about, and aims his rifle at Kuressa. Legathes and Xool gasp, but Yalena pulls out the pistol and aims.

Kuressa remains still at the other end of the hall.

"Kuressa," Rosek says. "Don't move."

Kuressa gurgles and suddenly splits in half. Four arms spout from the middle as three bodies emerge from the spitting guts and exploding lungs. As she rolls towards Rosek, he fires multiple times. After putting down the monster for good, Rosek turns to the others, but then he still aims his gun at Yalena.

Yalena frowns and says, "How dare you!"

After a few seconds, Yalena finally hears a crackle behind her. She studies the angle of Rosek's gun, realizes it goes over her shoulder, and she immediately leaps towards Rosek with a slide. She stops beside him and turns around with her gun up to see Xool being lifted off the ground by Legathes.

Xool spits blood out of his mouth as his shocked eyes still blink from the huge, white spike jutting out of his chest. In seconds, Xool falls limp as Legathes drops the dead body on the floor.

"Legathes," Rosek says. "What are you?!"

"I am Hynibrian," Legathes says and smirks. "I alone hold the higher power."

Rosek hisses air through his helmet. "Abomination. It's him!"

Yalena gasps and says, "How is that possible?! He's not—"

"Contaminated? No," Legathes says. "I will be what they are already."

"No," Yalena says. "Mater Ves is..."

"My home world," Legathes says. "You were killing my people, Rosek. That was not very wise."

Yalena partially hides behind Rosek. "Who sealed them away? Why?!"

Rosek does not move a muscle. "The Zeniths."

Legathes grimaces.

"Mater Ves," Rosek says. "That was not in your records."

"Nor would it be," Legathes says, "not when I'm the only one with the information. Why do you think I was sent on this mission, Rosek?"

Legathes takes a step closer and Rosek fires once. Yalena shudders and watches the wound seal shut.

"Rosek," Legathes says and smiles. "Do you trust me?"

Rosek reloads his gun.

"You disappoint me," Legathes says. "Both of you would be a great addition to the higher power. Ptol was too clean, so was Xool, but you two are perfect."

Rosek and Yalena start backing up.

Legathes holds out his glowing white hand. "Trust me. All of your pain will cease. All of your wounds will heal. Together, we can bring my people out of imprisonment and spread the higher power."

"Don't listen to him," Rosek says to Yalena and aims his gun. "He brings false light!"

Legathes smirks as the corners of his mouth split all the way to his ears. His skin splits along his neck and back as hands reach out from his spine. He slowly walks towards them and says, "Come with me."

Yalena screams, fires her gun twice, and blasts two massive holes into Legathes. He wails out as his head falls off to reveal ten faces inside of his neck hole. Rosek grabs Yalena by the wrist and they run down another hall.

Yalena keeps checking over her shoulder and says, "What do we do? He won't die!"

"He's a plague," Rosek says. "We must expel him!"

Yalena suddenly blinks rapidly and says, "The science lab! Go!"

Rosek and Yalena enter the science lab as Rosek seals the door and aims his gun. He hears Yalena rummaging around in the fridge and says, "What's the plan?!"

"Back on the *Manifest*," Yalena says, "Legathes called my personal treatment for ailments a poison."

"Well, can't say I can disagree with a walking famine."

"No," Yalena says. "He couldn't touch me. It was still in my blood. Whatever he is, he can't bind to us if we have elevated toxicity in our blood."

"No."

"Yes," Yalena says and smiles as she pulls out a large thermos. She spins off the lid, takes a whiff of the contents, and sighs. She glances to Rosek and she can feel his glare through the helmet. She frowns and says, "Fine. We'll shoot him with it."

Rosek nods as Yalena gathers needles full of the toxic drink and hands them to Rosek as Legathes slams into the door. He slides his hands along the clear door as his head rolls beneath his feet. His head blinks at them with a grin.

"You two are silly," Legathes says. "Hiding like children. Just trust me and all will be well! Open the door, Rosek, and I will free you of your torment."

Yalena aims her gun at the door. "You're the only sick person here!"

"You and Rosek are very sick," Legathes says. "So many imperfections. You, Yalena, are covered in scars inflicted by someone who said he loved you...and Rosek, oh Rosek...you thought I couldn't tell?"

Rosek's helmet hisses as he exhales. "Don't."

"You're worse than me," Legathes says and frowns. "Ask him, Yalena."

Rosek aims his gun at the door. "I'm done."

Legathes blinks as Rosek unloads hundreds of automatic mayhem on him and the hallway. Legathes howls as pieces of him fly off. Rosek points at Yalena and says, "Waste purge, now!"

Yalena hesitates as Legathes tries to put himself together.

Rosek turns to her and says, "Stay in the control center. I'll find you."

Yalena tosses him his pistol and runs.

Legathes builds back together, but he now looks like the others on Mater Ves. His bones are red and constantly oozing as his head rolls up into his own guts and settles there like a nightmare egg in a nest.

"I will have you," Legathes says. "And, before you are completely healed, you will watch me heal Yalena. I can slow the process, yes, and I can make it instantaneous. Together, we can heal all the people of DarkTime, even the Zeniths."

"They sealed you away," Rosek says and aims his gun. "Acceptable decision."

As Yalena runs down the hallway, she hears shots fire and she leaps down the control center tube. Crying as she enters the command, she hears the sirens as water rushes in all around her. Hyperventilating, Yalena feels the freezing waters rise past her knees

In the science lab hall, Rosek runs up a wall, fires, and Legathes crawls after him with twenty arms reaching for anything to touch and infect. Flipping down into the rising waters, Rosek starts removing his armor to become more fluid in an environment he was born to thrive.

Legathes continues to leap and thrash, but Rosek does not stop firing his gun. Leaving only his helmet on, Rosek's body shimmers along the sides with black scales on pale skin. He runs along the wall, builds momentum, and dives into the water like a shark as a fin pops up on his back. He swims through the water like an ancient crocodile, Legathes attempts to follow, and Rosek swims down into the lower levels of the ship.

Gurgling after him, Legathes uses all of his arms like an anemone to speed after Rosek's vulnerable body. Rosek continues to whip forward until he reaches the engine room. As he attempts to pry open the door, Legathes climbs down the stairs after him.

Pulling it open, Rosek swims inside as the gills on his neck exhale bubbles. Legathes follows, the water levels reach the ceiling, and Rosek leaps out of the water like a dolphin onto Legathes' back. He jabs him with dozens of needles, Legathes roars, and Rosek immediately leaps off of him and swims out of the room. Once he seals Legathes inside he enters a few commands on the door panel.

Inside the engine room, Legathes begins to deteriorate as the waters heat up inside the room. Suddenly, the engines turn red hot, the water boils, and Legathes dissolves as he cooks.

Up in the control center, Yalena takes in her last breath as the waters rise above her head. She glares at the control panels twenty feet down and swims to them. She tries to activate the water valves, but her fingers shake from oxygen deprivation. She clutches her chest, tries to resist the urge to take in air, and then she hears something bang into the control center. With a look of shock as she expels the last of her oxygen, Rosek takes hold of her and removes his helmet.

Half of his face is covered in Zenith biotech skin. From his right earlobe, across the bridge of his nose and hairless head, and down over his chin is veiny, black skin with synthetic, complex patterns that could only be mechanically constructed. One of his eyes is all black, even the sclera, and the other one is brilliant blue with a vertical black pupil. Horrible scars snake down his neck and into his chest, some of the organic staples breathing and moving with his pulse, and that's when she notices that half of the back of his head is gone. Part of his skull was removed, most likely while he was still awake, and inside is a mosaic prism net that sticks to his occipital lobe like plastic wrap.

Yalena clutches him back before she takes a watery breath, he kisses her, and he provides her with a new, full dose of oxygen. He breaks from her, swims to the control panels, and initiates the valve system.

Within minutes the rushing waters spin like a typhoon, Rosek grabs hold of Yalena, and he keeps her in his clutches as her rosy, red lips turn blue.

Once the waters flush out, Yalena gasps for air at the first chance and she holds onto Rosek as her body shakes. Soon, all that remains of the water is a slight dripping and Rosek stares out of the viewing monitors to see the last cooked bits of Legathes floating away into nowhere.

Shivering in his arms, Yalena looks at the monitor with Rosek and says, "Is h-he dead?"

"Not enough information," Rosek says and sighs. "Good enough."

Yalena collapses to the floor and Rosek joins her, still holding her, and she coughs. She stares up at him and says, "I have a confession."

Rosek smiles. "Yes?"

Yalena fishes the thermos out from behind her waist. "I saved some in case we have to make sure we're not infected."

Rosek snorts. "You're excused...just this once."

Yalena unscrews the cap and takes a large sip. She coughs hard and says, "Ptol! He drank ship fuel!"

"Hmm," Rosek says and takes a swig. "An adequate quantity to kill all the bacteria in my entire being."

Yalena quickly screws the cap back on. "Yes, I think I'll die if I drink anymore."

"So?"

Yalena blinks and drops the thermos. "What?"

"Your place?"

Yalena smirks. "Park in the back. This ride might scare my relatives."

Rosek laughs, the ship banks through a purple gas field, and Mater Ves glows in the distance. The Grakinium clouds swirl like swamp oil and the head of Legathes floats away as it continues to dissolve. The space waters halt only for a second, all sounds cease, and Legathes opens a single eye socket to reveal hundreds of eyes staring out in wallowing anger until they, too, eat each other until they break down into inert, black refuse, but Mater Ves remains.

Outpost Mission 883
Entry 37: Debriefing Summary

Rosek stands near the door inside a long, bleak room with only four windows that let in partial light from the heavy cloud cover. Standing at the last window, near a paper-ridden desk, Wendin shoves on his forest green hat over his messy hair and takes something out of his jacket.

For just a microsecond, Rosek tenses as his hand instinctually swings towards his pistol, but then he sees Wendin grab a small, silver canister and take a swig of the contents inside. Wendin glances once to Rosek and turns his attention back to the traffic outside.

"Apologies," Wendin says. "You've brought me a very disturbing and rather disappointing report. The Outpost will be upset that you destroyed an asset."

Rosek shifts his weight. "Hence my resignation."

Wendin snorts and takes another swig. He weakly shrugs and says, "Sorry, I…can't get over that part."

"If the Outpost can no longer recognize evil," Rosek says, "then I can no longer support the consortium."

"I understand," Wendin says and rubs his face with his free hand. "There's an expensive movement in the Outpost to test everyone Legathes came into contact with through touch. So far, no positive results. It appears…he kept his contagion to himself until he got back to Mater Ves."

"There is one question I have, Wendin."

"I'll grant it as a retirement present."

"Legathes said he was away when the Zeniths arrived," Rosek says and puts one hand on the door. "Where was he located when the Zeniths sealed Mater Ves?"

Wendin lowers his silver canister and turns to Rosek. A drop of the liquid inside runs down the rim of the canister and splashes onto the windowsill. Rosek uses his free hand to adjust his flak jacket near his heart and then returns to hovering it over his pistol.

Wendin blinks and says, "Rosek?"

Rosek watches the liquid on the windowsill suddenly flash with light. Before Wendin can make another heartbeat, Rosek has his lethal pistol aimed at him.

Wendin's expression slowly mutates as he grins. "I was willing to let you leave, for the sake of old ties, but now you jeopardize everything."

"You sent me to die!"

"I sent you," Wendin says as the corners of his face splits, "to be healed."

Rosek fires, but Wendin splits apart as organs fly out of his body like contagious projectiles. The door slams shut, organs hit the door and wall as they mutate into arms and fingers, and Rosek is sprinting down the hallway as all of the people in the building start to turn. The receptionist splits in half, three heads roll out of her exploding lungs, and Rosek makes a hard cut right through a window.

He hears the monsters screaming as he plummets, but he quickly spreads out his arms and legs to slow his descent as an Enidrome ship cuts in sideways out of the lower level fog, matches his fall, and slides underneath him so he can run along the flat top to the hatch. Once inside the ship, he feels the ship accelerate upwards and out of the atmosphere.

Rosek pauses at the new control center door, he waves his hand across and it opens to reveal Yalena in the driver's seat. She looks over her shoulder at him with a smile and says, "You called?"

Rosek removes the communicator from under his flak jacket and tosses it onto the dashboard. He sits in the seat beside her as a sigh hisses out of his helmet. He shakes his head and says, "Probability was moderate, but I did not take into account the entire Outpost Intelligence Agency being potentially infected."

Yalena enters a few commands and continues to drive. "Looks like I picked you up…just in time."

Rosek suddenly stands and sees something arrive on the monitors. He runs from the control center, down several hallways, and finally arrives to the newly installed viewing chamber. He stares through the clear walls and removes his helmet to make sure he is not hallucinating.

A gargantuan spear ship glitters with champagne and red coats of outer hull armor as thousands of small ships exit from massive docking bays in the center. As they swarm about the planet, other spear ships appear with great

Grakinium plates that are then welded together by the smaller ships. Within minutes, the entire planet is sealed.

Rosek stares out and says, "Zeniths."

Yalena steps into the viewing chamber. "They must have been there the entire time."

"They were waiting."

"Rosek," Yalena says and points back to the control center. "I'm getting Zenith chatter. They scanned the ship and let us through. Why?"

Rosek sighs and stares down at the ground.

Yalena blinks and says, "No…it's true."

Rosek looks up at her. "I never left."

Yalena runs up to him. "I'm still not afraid of you."

"My conditioning is only slightly broken," Rosek says, puts his helmet on, and takes hold of her narrow shoulders, "but that's enough to save you. The ship is yours. I will…never forget you, Yalena."

Yalena kisses his helmet with her red lips before he is suddenly gone. Sinking onto the bench and sighing, Yalena watches the Zenith ships stop sealing the planet and disappear. They blur in and out of time, distort, and like a mirage they merely vanish. The Zenith chatter echoes down the halls, but then it cuts off. She fishes a small, silver container from her space suit and unscrews the cap.

"The one man I like," Yalena says and takes a swig. She dramatically exhales with a long sigh. "A Zenith. Psh, figures."

Made in the USA
Columbia, SC
23 April 2023